G.H.O.S.T. SQUAD

The CREEPY CATHEDRAL

By Brittany Canasi

Illustrated by Katie Wood

Rourke
Educational Media
rourkeeducationalmedia.com

www.rourkeeducationalmedia.com

PHOTO CREDITS: pg 45 ©Nowhereman86/wikipedia

Edited by: Keli Sipperley
Cover layout by: Tara Raymo
Interior layout by: Kathy Walsh
Cover and Interior Illustrations by: Katie Wood

Library of Congress PCN Data

The Creepy Cathedral / Brittany Canasi
(G.H.O.S.T. Squad)
ISBN 978-1-68342-342-3 (hard cover)(alk. paper)
ISBN 978-1-68342-438-3 (soft cover)
ISBN 978-1-68342-508-3 (e-Book)
Library of Congress Control Number: 2017931187

Printed in the United States of America,
North Mankato, Minnesota

All cheer. No fear. That's the G.H.O.S.T Squad's motto. These girls hunting oddities and supernatural things are always up to something, whether it's cheerleading practice, pep rallies, or investigating spooks.

Mags, Scarlett, and Luna have built a business helping the haunted. And, along with Scarlett's service dog, Dakota, they're scaring up a lot of fun in the process. Each book in the G.H.O.S.T Squad series is self-contained, so they don't have to be read in any particular order. And every book is teeming with back matter, including an explainer section on paranormal studies, information about a real reportedly haunted location like that in the story, author interviews, and further reading suggestions.

Meet the Authors:
Brittany Canasi and K.A. Robertson have wanted to collaborate on a fiction series for years. And now they have! They worked together to develop the characters and concepts that drive the G.H.O.S.T Squad series, then they each wrote their books based on those ideas, helping each other shape their manuscripts along the way.

Meet the Illustrator:
Katie Woods' talent and commitment to bringing the G.H.O.S.T Squad characters to life were invaluable to the series. Katie is never happier than when she is drawing, and is living her dream as a freelance illustrator. She works happily from her studio in Leicester, England, and her work is published all over the world.

"The wonderful characters in this book have been an endless source of delight and inspiration. It has been so exciting to be part of the G.H.O.S.T Squad team and find out what adventures these girls will encounter next!" Katie says.

Brittany, K.A., Katie and the entire Rourke team hope these books tickle your funny bone and scare you silly!

Happy reading,
Rourke Educational Media

Meet the
G.H.O.S.T. Squad

*(Girls Hunting Oddities
& Supernatural Things)*

Luna: Discovered her psychic abilities in third grade, when a spirit warned her about the vegetables hidden under her pizza cheese. That night she also discovered her mother, a popular (and totally embarrassing) psychic on TV, is not psychic at all.

Other: Loves soccer and cheerleading. Hates broccoli.

Mags: Short for Magdeline. Her family has lived in New Orleans since it was founded in 1718. They know pretty much everything about everyone. And if they don't know, Mags knows how to dig up the dirt. Mags has a brain full of history knowledge and she's not afraid to use it.

Other: Best back tuck on the cheer squad. Afraid of clowns and pufferfish. (Don't ask why, she won't talk about it.)

Scarlett: Cheer captain, skeptic, and technology genius. Enjoys code cracking, hacking, and teaching her service dog, Dakota, strange tricks. Lost her lower leg in an accident. Became gymnast and cheerleader soon after.

Other: Founded G.H.O.S.T. Squad in third grade after Luna told her about the invisible hero who saved her from a mouthful of greens. Still doesn't totally believe in ghosts. Still totally loves ghost hunting.

Dakota: Labrador. Scarlett's service dog. Recently learned to skateboard and sneeze on command. But not at the same time. Yet.

Other: Can smell ghosts. Will do anything for bacon.

Case ID: Creep1

Location: Our Lady of Divine Joy church

Background:
Reports of a spirit disturbing churchgoers. Has happened on and off for over twenty years. Tourists find it fascinating. Wedding planners do not.

Reported Activity:

- Spontaneous pipe organ playing
- Hanging tapestries moving
- Cold breezes

Possible causes:

- Bad wiring to organ?
- Air conditioning blowing too hard?
- Someone has a bad cold and SNEEZES EVERYWHERE EWWWW

Table of Contents

Chapter 1
A New Client

"Old churches give me the creeps. How much longer until this lady shows up?," Mags said, bending down to pet Dakota. The yellow Labrador was technically Scarlett's service dog, but she was a huge fan of anyone who wanted to give her a scratch behind the ears.

"Hopefully soon," Luna said. "My mom's show is tonight. She's making me help again."

"Think she'll talk to an actual ghost this time, or is she gonna keep pulling people's legs?" Scarlett said, wiggling her eyebrows up and down as she made a big deal of jiggling her prosthetic leg.

"You're going to comedy jail," Luna said.

A bright red convertible pulled up along the side of the road. A woman in a fur-lined vest and big sunglasses got out and approached the entrance of Our Lady of Divine Joy church.

Scarlett let out a low whistle.

"Bet it's going to be a really nice wedding,"

she said.

"Hi, girls," the woman said. She pushed her sunglasses on top of her head and smiled warmly at them.

"You must be Violet," Mags said, walking over to the woman. *Firm handshake, eye contact, friendly smile.* Mags could hear her Mamere's commands of how a successful young lady should conduct herself.

"I'm so sorry I'm late, I had a disaster with the caterer. They were trying to serve chicken at my wedding. Can you imagine?" she said.

"Sometimes my mom brings fried chicken home after work. It's actually pretty good," Scarlett said. Dakota's ears perked up, as if someone might offer her a piece.

"So, you've got a wedding coming up," Mags said, steering the talk away from fried food. "And you have a problem with... a ghost?"

"Yes, I'd heard this place is haunted, but I didn't realize it was quite so bad until we started looking at it for the wedding. And I couldn't choose any other place. It's where my grandmother got married. She died right after I got engaged, and I ... I want it to seem like she's there. With us."

Scarlett looked over at Luna, whose lower lip was quivering. As the group's medium, she felt things way more than most people. Ghost feelings, people feelings. Maybe one day she might feel Dakota's feelings. Scarlett nudged her dog gently in Luna's direction, and Dakota took to her temporary duty as Luna's comforter. Luna gave the dog a glassy-eyed smile and a scratch under the chin.

"Well, why don't we go inside and see what we're working with?" Mags said to Violet. She turned and motioned for Violet to lead the way.

"Oh no, I can't go back in there," she said. "Not after last time. I still have nightmares about that pipe organ. And the water stains from the holy water never came out of my suede boots. I just can't."

"She's not trying to win sympathy points with that, is she?" Scarlett mumbled to Luna as Violet walked quickly back to her car.

"Thank you, girls, for helping! I know you'll save the day!" she yelled over her shoulder as the convertible drove off.

"Can we tell her she has to give us her car if we get rid of this ghost?" Luna said.

"We can't drive for years," Mags said.

"But the best things are worth waiting for," Luna said, her eyes dreamy.

G.H.O.S.T Squad
@G.H.O.S.T Squad

Squawk-What's going on?

@NewOrleansGazette:
@NewOrleans biggest socialite @VioletDallier 2 marry @ **Our Lady of Divine Joy.** *Is the ghost invited?!*

@JamezAllSaintz:
@NewOrleansGazette if the ghost is going, *it'll be the only guest! LOL!*

@BaudinKnowsBest:
@JamezAllSaintz don't make me call your momma and tell her ur being ugly on the Internet again.

@JamezAllSaintz:
@BaudinKnowsBest *NO PLZ DON'T* – I TAKE IT BACK : * * (

Chapter 2
Bridezilla?

The G.H.O.S.T. Squad walked through the heavy front doors of the church, passed through the front lobby, and entered the main part of the church.

"Is someone going to yell at us for being here?" Luna asked.

"Not if we make it quick. The priest takes a thirty minute break every day. He just left," Mags said.

Luna stopped walking.

"Oh, man. I feel something," she said.

"It's probably me. I'm starving," Scarlett said. Dakota barked in agreement.

"Hilarious. No, it feels … sad. But it's going away I think."

"Great! Job's already done. Let's head out of here," Scarlett said, clapping her hands.

The tapestries on the wall flapped.

"Whoa. I didn't clap that hard," Scarlett said. Dakota hid behind her and whimpered.

"It's the ghost, isn't it?" Mags said. "Luna, say something to it." Mags dug through her backpack and pulled out an EMF reader and heat-sensing goggles. The former from Luna's mother, the latter from a very satisfied client.

Mags strapped on the heat-sensing goggles and held out the EMF meter to Scarlett.

Luna closed her eyes and tried to find the sad feeling again. The cold, lonely feeling came back, making her chest feel heavy. She concentrated on it and racked her brain for what to say.

Cheer up?

Why are you so sad?

Are you the reason this church smells like moldy books?

"Hello, whoever you are," Luna said out loud. "We're here to help you move on. We want to know why you're here, so we can figure out how you can rest for good. Give us a sign."

Scarlett looked down at the EMF meter, but it wasn't moving. She looked over at Mags, who was looking around wildly, trying to find something out of the ordinary. Judging by the fact that she didn't stop, Scarlett was pretty

sure she wasn't having any better luck.

"It's not working, Luna," Scarlett whispered.

"Mister or Missus Ghost?" Mags said. "Are you there?"

"Is that really how we speak to spirits, Mags?" Luna hissed. "How long have we been doing this?"

"What? *History Mystery* has a new episode tonight, and I want to wrap up here before I miss it," Mags said, holding up her hands in surrender.

There was a high-pitched clicking sound, signaling that the EMF meter detected a spike in the electromagnetic field. In paranormal research, those spikes can mean a ghost is nearby.

"Holy cow, it actually worked. These numbers are spiking like crazy," Scarlett said, pointing to the flashing lights on the device.

Mags looked around the room, trying to find visual evidence of a spirit. She saw red outlines of her friends and Dakota, room temperature everywhere else. She looked toward one of the windows, where some of the tapestries hung.

And in the corner of the church, not all that

far from them, was a small ball of blue light, hovering in the air.

"I think I found it," she whispered.

She turned to look at the girls, then back at the ball. The ball darted away from the corner to the other side of the church, then the other, then back and forth from either end of the church. Mags ripped off the goggles to find the tapestries flying wildly on their hooks. One fell to the ground with a loud crash.

Dakota barked, hid behind Scarlett, then came out and barked again, then returned to her hiding spot.

"Guys, I think it's time to cut and run," Mags said. "This spirit seems—"

But the girls never heard the end of Mags' sentence. Because at that moment, the church's very loud, very intense organ began playing.

The girls slapped their hands over their ears, and Dakota put her paw over her face. The papers on the church bulletin began flapping like the tapestries, some flying around the room. The calendar pinned to the board fluttered, each month ripping off the wall, one by one: *March. April. May. June. July.*

The next page shook, but did not tear off. *August.*

Chapter 3
Ring It In

Investigation Results:
- Ghost is sad
- Ghost plays organ???
- Ghost plays organ VERY LOUD! WHY???
- Messed with events board. August on calendar?
- Dakota needs to go on a bathroom break before ghost hunting

Possible Causes:
- electrical issues cause pipe organ to play?
- stranger snuck in and played while we were there?
- faulty a/c blew too hard?
- THESE ARE ALL PRETTY WEAK
- I'M STRUGGLING HERE OK?? IT WAS PROBS A GHOST
- IT WAS DEF A GHOST

The girls piled in the car waiting for them outside. Mags' grandmother, Mamere, had offered to pick them up. The group needed some answers, and no one was better for gossip than her grandmother. There was just one problem: Mamere was a terrifying driver.

Mags was thrown against the passenger door as the car took a sharp right turn, then a left, the tires screeching in protest.

The group eventually made it safely to an outdoor cafe a couple of miles away. Scarlett, who looked a little green in the face from the drive over, only ordered a Sprite and picked at the bread on the table.

Mags told her Mamere everything they'd learned so far: the calendar, the pipe organ, the sadness Luna felt.

"You forgot the song," Scarlett said, slowly gaining color back in her face.

"What song?" Mags asked.

"The song the pipe organ played. It was 'Here Comes the Bride'."

"You're right," Mags said. Mags hadn't recognized the song at first. And to be honest, her ears hurt too much from its volume to think about it at the time.

"Well, that's all very interesting," Mamere said. "A woman named Augusta Chadwick used to play the organ there years ago."

"Mags, August!" Luna whispered. "The calendar stopped at August!"

Scarlett pulled her tablet from her backpack. She opened the Zoogle search page and typed *Augusta Chadwick*.

The top result was a decades-old obituary. Scarlett clicked on the link and turned the tablet so Mags and Luna could see.

𝔑𝔢𝔴 𝔒𝔯𝔩𝔢𝔞𝔫𝔰 𝔊𝔞𝔷𝔢𝔱𝔱𝔢

Beloved Organ Player Passes after Long Battle with Pneumonia

originally published May 27th, 1985

Augusta Chadwick, the beloved organ player at Our Lady of Divine Joy, passed away after a months-long battle with pneumonia.

Chadwick had originally contracted the illness after her ill-fated wedding day, where she was famously left at the altar by William Beauregard, noted ladies man and all-around huge jerk. (editor's note: status of "jerk" has not been independently verified, but the ladies man thing is pretty solid.)

In her final hours, Chadwick could be heard mumbling, "The ring. Where's the ring?" Sources believe she was referring to her wedding ring, which disappeared along with Beauregard.

Services will be held at Our Lady of Divine Joy on Sunday. In lieu of flowers, the family requests donations to the church.

"Think we can get that ring back?" Mags asked. "That may be what's keeping her around. It's unfinished business."

"She's got a niece that lives not too far from here. I'm sure she'd love to have it," Mamere said.

Scarlett was tapping away on her tablet, eyebrows furrowed in concentration.

"Found him. Well, kind of."

"Who?" Mags asked.

"William Beauregard. Well, where he used to live, at least. He died ten years ago. Boating accident. Wife left him just before that, according to these divorce records. Looks like she still lives in Gulfport, Mississippi. Family's got a huge shrimping business there."

"You can find all that information on that thing?" Mamere asked, pointing to Scarlett's tablet.

"I got a subscription to a pretty powerful database for my birthday. I can find out pretty much anything about anyone," Scarlett said, sneaking a piece of bread to Dakota, who was very happy to take it.

"Peculiar choice for a birthday present,"

Mamere mumbled as she took a sip from her iced tea.

"What are the odds she kept the ring? And would she be willing to give it back?" Mags asked.

"Why don't you girls leave that to me," Mamere said. "I can be very, very persuasive when I need to be."

"You gonna whack her, Mamere?" Mags teased.

"A lady never reveals her methods, darling," Mamere said slyly.

"Why don't we finish up here and take a drive over there? It's a beautiful day for a road trip!" Mamere said.

Scarlett pleaded silently with Mags: *Please, please, please do not make me get back into that car for longer than it takes her to drop us at home. The drive here nearly killed me.*

Mags picked up on her cry for help and gave her grandmother a sweet smile.

"We have a basketball game to cheer for Monday, and we're still learning our new routine. Plus, wouldn't we get in the way while you worked your magic? Or, you know, end up as witnesses?"

Scarlett and Luna barely muffled their sighs of relief.

"All right, all right. I'll be there and back in a couple of hours."

"Mamere, doesn't it take an hour and a half just to get there?"

Her grandmother looked back at her with a mischievous smile that said, *Not the way I drive, sweetheart.*

Chapter 4
OOPS, Made YOU Spook

Mamere:
On the way

Mags
u driving? stop texting!!

Mamere:
2 mins away. This is Grace
texting for Mrs. Baudin

Mags:
Grace who????

"Sounds like Mamere has another victim in the passenger seat," Mags said as they waited outside Our Lady of Divine Joy.

"I love your grandmother, but she's a menace

to society in that car," Scarlett said.

"I think I hear her," Luna said.

The sound of screeching tires got louder as they saw Mags' grandmother round the corner in her bright white town car. She sped down the street and skidded to a stop in front of the church.

"That was awesome," Luna said, laughing.

"Don't encourage her," Mags mumbled.

Mamere got out of the car. She gestured for the woman in the passenger seat to join her.

"This is Grace Redding. She's Augusta Chadwick's niece, and a fine young lady."

Grace smiled tentatively at the group and shook each of their hands shyly. She looked queasy, too. She'd clearly gotten the full *Mamere's Wild Ride* experience.

"I heard what you girls are doing. I want to help if I can. I never got to meet my Aunt Augusta, but I've only heard great things about her. If that's her in there, I just want her to be happy," she said.

"That's our goal. To help her move on," Luna said.

"Also, so our client can get married here without people peeing their pants when the place goes all spooky again," said Scarlett. Mags elbowed her in the side, and she winced.

"Sorry," Mags said to Grace.

Grace smiled sweetly at Scarlett, but her eyes widened with fear.

Great, Scarlett spooked the girl, Luna thought.

"I've got something else you all should probably see. Especially you, Grace. From my trip over to Gulfport," Mamere said.

"Gulfport?" Grace asked. But the entire G.H.O.S.T. Squad, Dakota included, perked up. They knew what was coming next. Or at least, they hoped they did.

Mags' grandmother pulled out an envelope from her purse and gave it to Grace.

"Careful with what's inside. She wrote you a note, too."

"Who did?" Grace asked.

She opened the envelope and let out a small gasp when she pulled out a ring. It rested on the top part of her pointer finger as she admired the braided platinum band and the single diamond in the middle. She opened the note and read it aloud.

~ Mrs. Eliza Wagner ~

Dearest Grace,

Mrs. Baudin just told me the most dreadful story about your dear Aunt Augusta. I am sorry to say it doesn't surprise me in the least. William was an awful husband, and I was too young and dumb at the time to realize it.

I'm also sorry to hear that the ring I wore during our brief, unhappy marriage belonged to your aunt. I almost sold it after we divorced, but something told me to keep it. I now know why.

Please have it. It only reminds me of my nasty ex-husband. I trust it'll remind you of your dear aunt instead.

Your friend,
Eliza

"I bet she has a lot of money if she's just giving diamonds away like that," Scarlett said.

"Scarlett!" Luna and Mags said at the same time.

"What? I'm just saying," Scarlett mumbled, ruffling Dakota's fur.

Chapter 5
Family Bonds

Case updates
Possible solution:
Step 1: Niece meets ~~ghost aunt~~ spirit of aunt
Step 2: Show ring has been returned (Scarlett)
Step 3: We all go home and hopefully my mom makes brownies tonight

Luna, Mags, Scarlett, and Dakota led the way into Our Lady of Divine Joy. Grace followed close behind. Past the lobby, Luna grabbed onto the large wooden door that led into the main part of the church.

"Wait," Grace said, panic in her voice.

The three of them looked back at Grace. Dakota wagged her tail, wondering if they were

about to play a game: *Simon says... go find a ghost!*

"I think I should stay out here," Grace said in a shaky voice. "I've, well, I've never seen an actual ghost before, aunt or not. I don't want to be unhelpful, but I'm not sure I can handle it. I'll be right here while you guys are in there."

Scarlett, Luna, and Mags looked at each other in silent conversation. Do we grab her and force her into the church? Probably not. Kidnapping, even if it's only a few yards away, could be bad for business.

"If you want," Luna said. "We'll be out in a moment."

"Here, take this," Grace said, handing over the ring. "Maybe it'll help if she can see it? Can ghosts see?"

"It definitely doesn't hurt," Luna said, taking the ring. The three girls turned back toward the door and let Dakota lead the way in. After discussing (arguing) where they should be when they talked to Augusta, they decided on the pipe organ. If she was the church's organ player, she probably had a lot of happy memories there.

Mags powered on the EMF meter. Click, click, click. The meter spiked immediately.

"Oh, she's definitely here. Look at this thing," Mags said.

"I feel her," Luna whispered. "Way more than I did last time. I wonder if she knows about the ring."

"Well, ask her," Scarlett said.

"Augusta? We heard about your story, and we want to help you. We found your ring," Luna said. Mags opened her palm and held out the ring.

"Your niece, Grace, is just outside. She has the ring, and it'll stay in your family, where it belongs," Luna said.

A long, low note came from the pipe organ. Dakota covered her eyes with one paw.

Three more notes played simultaneously on the organ, like someone was just making noise, rather than playing a song. Then another three. Louder this time.

"You guys, she's not happy. I don't think she believes us about her niece."

"Go grab her!" Scarlett yelled to Mags.

Mags ran through the church and into the lobby. Grace sat in a chair by the door. Her hands were tightly folded together in her lap. She looked extremely pale.

"That's her, isn't it?" Grace said.

"Yes. I really need your help or none of this is going to work," Mags said, trying to catch her breath. It was a good reminder to not skip laps at cheer practice.

"All right, I'll help," Grace said.

The two of them rushed into the fray, the organ still making its awful blasts of noise. Scarlett, Luna, and Dakota sat there with looks on their faces that said, *This is the least amount of fun we've ever had.*

"Aunt Augusta? It's Grace," she said quietly. The sounds didn't stop.

"You're gonna have to speak louder!" Mags yelled over the noise.

"Aunt Augusta!" Grace bellowed. The organ stopped playing, and her voice echoed through the church.

"Aunt Augusta, it's your niece, Grace. I'm your only living relative now that Momma passed on last year," she said.

The church stayed silent.

"She's listening," Luna whispered.

"Aunt Augusta, I'm so sorry for what happened to you all those years ago, and I'm sorry William took your ring. But I have it back now, and it will go to my daughter, and her daughter, and it'll stay in the family forever. Like a part of you is always with us. You should be at peace, Aunt Augusta. You should move on. Let this place be as joyful as it was for you when you played here. Please."

A soft breeze passed by the girls.

Scarlett stepped forward and slapped her hands on her thighs.

"All right, we good here? Is she gone?"

"You're a wizard with words and sensitivity," Mags said.

"She's gone. I don't feel her anymore," Luna said.

"That was the scariest thing I've ever done, even if it was my aunt I was talking to. How do you guys do this all the time?" Grace asked.

"Easy. College applications. Also the occasional cash reward," Scarlett said.

Chapter 6
School Spirit

"All right ladies, let's bring it in for some announcements," Coach said.

The entire cheer squad left their formations and gathered around. Dakota stood next to the coach, waiting for Scarlett to ask for assistance.

"Did you hear about Violet's wedding?" Mags whispered to Luna and Scarlett. "They had nine chocolate fountains, and she got walked down the aisle on an actual horse that she owned."

"Let me guess, your grandmother was invited?" Scarlett asked.

"Sure was," Mags said.

"That woman is friends with everyone. We saved the wedding, and she got nine chocolate fountains," Luna said.

"Shhhh. Ladies, ladies. I have some great news for everyone," Coach said. "We received a large donation from a Miss Violet Dallier, and it's enough to get us those new warm-up suits.

Plus, new t-shirts to wear to school on game days."

The squad cheered. *New stuff. Free new stuff. Awesome free new stuff!*

"That's way cooler than chocolate fountains," Mags said. Luna nodded in agreement.

"Maybe. But I'm definitely getting a chocolate fountain for my next birthday party," Scarlett said.

What is Paranormal Research?

Something that lies outside normal experience or scientific explanation is considered paranormal. When people claim to sense or see ghosts, that is a paranormal experience. Science has not been able to prove the existence of ghosts. On the other hand, there's no conclusive evidence that they don't exist, either.

Paranormal researchers are not necessarily scientists. Scientists have much stricter guidelines for performing experiments that can be tested and retested. Paranormal researchers use the tools available to them to collect evidence, such as electronic voice phenomena (EVP), and electromagnetic field (EMF) readings. They also rely on personal accounts of witnesses who think they are experiencing paranormal activity, and their own experiences in a haunted location. Researching a location's history is also a critical part of paranormal research. An investigator will gather information about the people and events associated with a place to determine if there is a reason for the paranormal activity to occur, such as a sudden death or a traumatic event. Proving the existence of a ghost in a way that can be tested and retested in a scientific manner is quite tricky, since no one's figured out how to catch one yet!

A "Real" Haunted Cathedral

The St. Louis Cathedral Basilica in New Orleans, right across from Jackson Square, is home to quite a few spooky tenants. There have been four different churches in the spot where it stands. Even though the older churches aren't around anymore, their former members might be.

Pere Antoine (1748 – 1829), a church monk, is said to still wander the grounds. Witnesses claim they've seen him in his full human form. He sometimes wanders the church gardens or Pere Antoine's Alley. If you see a tall man with a long, white beard wandering around St. Louis Cathedral reading a book of prayers, you may be looking at Pere Antoine!

Other former members of St. Louis Cathedral stick around because of past regrets. Marie Laveau (1801 – 1881), a famous voodoo queen, is claimed to have stuck around long after her death, too. People say they've spotted her in the cemetery practicing voodoo and praying for forgiveness in the church.

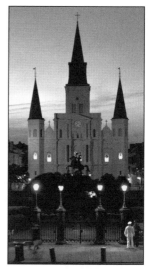

New Orleans has several ghost tours available, and St. Louis Cathedral is one of their most important stops!

Many of the original graves at St. Louis Cathedral were unmarked, and bones are sometimes found during construction projects.

45

What is a Medium?

In the G.H.O.S.T Squad series, Luna is described as a medium, or sensitive. This means she can tune into the energy of spirits around her, to feel their emotions and communicate with them. Not all people who claim to be psychic are mediums. Some psychics only claim to see into the past and/or future. A medium is defined specifically as someone who claims to communicate with the spirits of people who have passed away. Like ghosts, science hasn't proven these abilities really exist, but they haven't disproven their existence either.

Q & A with Brittany Canasi

Q: *What interests you about ghost stories?*
A: Ghosts represent the unknown, which is what makes them scary! Every ghost has a different story and a different reason for not crossing over to the other side. No two ghost stories are identical.

Q: *What is the most haunted place you've ever visited?*
A: There is a cemetery in Los Angeles that shows movies in the summer. People gather in a grassy field away from the graves and have picnics. There have been reports of a woman crying by a lake, as well as people appearing in older clothing. Cemetery employees say they've seen spirits walk through walls!

Test Your Reading Comprehension!

1. Why is Dakota part of the G.H.O.S.T. Squad?

2. Who was haunting Our Lady of Divine Joy?

3. How did Mamere help the G.H.O.S.T. Squad?

4. Why does the G.H.O.S.T. Squad need to find the ring?

5. What did the G.H.O.S.T. Squad receive for getting rid of the ghost?

Further Reading

For more information, check out your local library for books on ghost lore. Many books focus on specific regions. You may discover some haunts in your own hometown! You can also look for books on paranormal research and equipment such as electromagnetic field (EMF) detectors. If you're interested in a specific place that's rumored to be haunted, dig into public records and periodicals such as old local newspapers to see what you can find out about the people who once lived or worked there. Is there a mystery to be solved that might explain reports of a haunting? Try to solve it!